The Daring Rescue

L·U·C·Y and the Magic Loom

The Daring Rescue

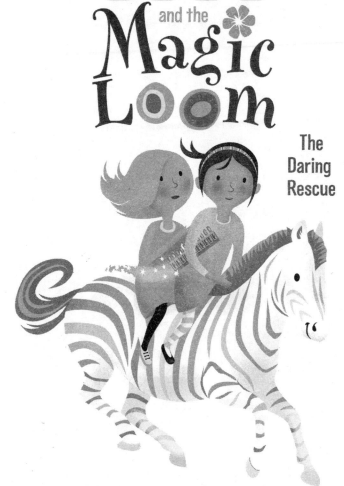

A Rainbow Loomer's Adventure Story
by Madeline Downest

SKY PONY PRESS
NEW YORK

Sky Pony Press books may be purchased in bulk at special discounts for sales promotion, corporate gifts, fund-raising, or educational purposes. Special editions can also be created to specifications. For details, contact the Special Sales Department, Sky Pony Press, 307 West 36th Street, 11th Floor, New York, NY 10018 or info@skyhorsepublishing.com.

Sky Pony® is a registered trademark of Skyhorse Publishing, Inc.®, a Delaware corporation.

Visit our website at www.skyponypress.com.

10 9 8 7 6 5 4 3 2

Library of Congress Cataloging-in-Publication Data

Downest, Madeline.
  Lucy and the magic loom : the daring rescue story / Madeline Downest.
    pages cm. -- (A rainbow loomer's adventure story ; 2)
  Summary: Twelve-year-old Lucy must find a way to re-enter the enchanted world after her best friend misuses the magic loom and disappears.
  ISBN 978-1-63450-215-3 (pb : alk. paper) [1. Rescues--Fiction. 2. Magic--Fiction. 3. Friendship--Fiction. 4. Adventure and adventurers--Fiction.] I. Title. II. Title: Daring rescue story.
  PZ7.1.D688Lu 2016
  [Fic]--dc23
2015000894

Ebook ISBN: 978-1-63450-894-0

Cover design and illustration by Jan Gerardi

Printed in Canada

The
Daring
Rescue

Chapter One

Lucy Stillwater-Smith was sitting on her bed, puffy-eyed and sniffling. Her very best friend, Alyssa, had moved to America just one year ago and was visiting Lucy for the summer. But today was the day Lucy had been dreading, when Alyssa would fly back across the wide Atlantic Ocean to New York City. Lucy knew that the old white stone town house at 163 Terrier Square would not be the same.

The door creaked open. Lucy looked up and saw two big brown eyes and a splash of gold hair peering at her through the crack in the door. "Alyssa?" Alyssa came into the room and flung her arms around Lucy. The two girls had spent the summer visiting all of Alyssa's favorite spots in London; one night they got dressed up and went to a fancy musical, and they took day trips to hilly parts of the countryside. They gorged on their favorite snacks, like curry chips and chocolate biscuits, and every night they stayed up late, giggling under an elaborate fort made of sheets in Lucy's bedroom.

"I'm going to miss you, too!" Alyssa said before Lucy could try to explain her puffy eyes. They hugged each other tightly, and suddenly Lucy felt a pinch on her head.

"Ouch! Your bracelet is stuck in my hair!" They had made each other elastic friendship bracelets, which were the best and by far the most beautiful of any they had ever seen. But they could get caught on things. Very carefully, Alyssa unhooked the bracelet's plastic clasp and removed it from the tangles in Lucy's brown hair.

Alyssa fiddled with the clasp to get the friendship bracelet back on her wrist. "Just make a knot, it'll be faster," said Lucy. She tied a knot and the two girls put their bracelets next to each other and smiled. "You can *never* take yours off, got it?"

Alyssa's eyes widened. "Like that would ever happen! Every day we'll look at our wrists and know the other person is looking too, and we'll be friends forever."

"Knock, knock, ladies—incoming!" Miss Abigail Sanders bustled into the bedroom and dropped a pile of clean laundry onto the bed. "Oh, you darlings," Abigail said with a frown when she noticed the pile of tissues that Lucy had collected on her bed. "I know you're going to miss each other, but just think of all the fun you've had this summer!"

"I don't want Alyssa to go, Abigail! It's not fair—can't she stay?"

"Can't I? Can't I stay?" Alyssa chimed in.

Abigail's eyes twinkled. "I think Alyssa's parents might have something to say about that. How about some tea and biscuits before you get ready for your flight? Will that help?" The girls' moods instantly shifted and they nodded approvingly. Abigail always knew how to make everything better. She had taken care of Lucy for Lucy's whole life, and while Lucy could now do basically everything on her own, Abigail was still wonderful for all of the little things, like knowing which snacks to buy, and big things, too, like making sure the Doctors didn't forget to go to Lucy's recitals.

"The Doctors" were Lucy's parents. Dr. Stillwater was her dad. He researched cures for all kinds of infectious diseases, with a particular emphasis on the gross ones. Dr. Smith was her mum, and she worked in a hospital that helped children who had cancer. Lucy loved them both to the moon and back, but they were also very important people with very important jobs, which meant that Lucy didn't get to see them all that often.

Abigail floated out of the room and her voice carried from the hallway as she said she'd start the teakettle. Lucy jumped off the bed and hopped over Alyssa's nearly full suitcase toward the door. "Are you coming, Alyssa?" Alyssa's eyes were caught on something on the bookshelf, and she murmured distractedly about needing to put a couple more things in her suitcase. "Okay, whatever, I'll be downstairs but just hurry up!"

Lucy pranced around the kitchen, excited for tea and biscuits. Abigail had put out a plate already, and Lucy was getting antsy waiting for Alyssa. After several minutes, the teakettle shrieked and Lucy realized that Alyssa was still not downstairs.

"*ALYSSAAAAA!*" She went to the bottom of the stairs. "Come on—this is your last opportunity for English tea! American tea is just *terrible!*" She waited to hear a giggle from Alyssa, but there was no response.

Lucy started up the stairs. "Alyssa? We can finish packing later." Lucy pushed open her bedroom door but there was no one there. She checked every room on the floor, all of which were empty. She took a seat on her bed, checking her phone to see if Alyssa had texted her. Maybe this was a joke.

In the corner of her room, something caught her eye. Alyssa's friendship bracelet lay undone on the floor, right next to the spot where Lucy kept her magic loom secretly stowed away. She studied the bracelet, then knelt down beside the bookshelf and scoured through its contents. A year ago, Lucy had received a magical Rainbow Loom in the mail, one that brought her to another world of magical creatures. She had used her Rainbow Loom skills to make her way through the world and help a new friend. But as she searched her shelf, the magic loom was gone, and so was her best friend.

Chapter Two

Lucy was in a panic. The magic loom was very special. Last year when the package came in the mail, it was addressed to someone other than her. Lucy had opened it anyway, which had led to Lucy being grounded, because you're not supposed to open mail that isn't yours. Lucy had crept into her parents' room where her mum had stowed the package anyway, and an amazing thing had happened: the magic loom had buzzed and glowed as soon as she touched it, and Lucy knew it *must* belong to her. To her wonder, it brought her through the bookcase and into an astonishing world filled with magical creatures. She learned to use the magic loom in incredible ways, from constructing fantastical wings to stringing bridges across vast gorges.

The magic loom was special, indeed, and Lucy had written to Alyssa to tell her all about it.

Alyssa had read Lucy's tales in earnest and written hastily back, eager for more detail of everything the magic loom had to offer. Lucy knew that with the loom's incredible power, though, also came incredible danger. The magical world was a beautiful place with helpful creatures, but it also held secrets and challenges that could only be solved with intricate skill and understanding of the loom's powers. Lucy had told Alyssa how she had crossed over to the magical world through the bookcase in her parents' office. But her parents' office was totally off limits!

"Girls, are you coming down for tea?" Abigail called from below. Lucy did her best impression of Alyssa's laughter and yelled down, "One more minute, we're just washing up!" Lucy winced as she lied to Abigail. She crept up the stairs to the Doctors' third floor office, tiptoeing to avoid each of the floorboards that she knew would creak under her feet. Cautiously peering around the doorway, Lucy stepped into the room. The Doctors' office had two scrupulously tidy desks for when they needed to do work from home, a wall of six completely full bookcases, and a collection of photos of Lucy from every age scattered around the room. But what caught Lucy's eye was one huge, ridiculous, gigantic, messy, dusty, mountainous, disastrous problem: one of the *massive* bookcases was facedown on the ground, with all of its contents strewn about the room.

Lucy's heart sank. This could only mean one thing. Well, actually, two things: the first was that she would most certainly be grounded for eternity for the mess in front of her, and the second was that Alyssa had without a doubt gone to the magical realm and taken the golden loom with her. This was terrible! The bookcase was Lucy's only way to the magic realm, and the only way to get through was with the magic loom! Would Alyssa ever return without Lucy's help? What if she could never get back? Lucy needed to cross over and help Alyssa. She slumped down on the window seat of the Doctors' room, anxious and full of worry. She leaned her head against the cool glass window, and started to choke up at the idea that her friend might be gone forever.

In the corner of her eye, she saw a shape move outside the window. Lucy snapped up; it was Mrs. Gloucester! She was the only other person who knew about the portal. Last year, Mrs. Gloucester had helped Lucy when she wasn't sure she could find her way home from the magical realm. Lucy watched as Mrs. Gloucester fiddled with her keys to get into her car. Where was she going? Lucy began rapping on the window loudly, waving to try and make herself known. "Mrs. Gloucester! Mrs. Gloucester, I need to talk with you!" But the old woman couldn't hear her from so high up. Lucy started to panic; there was no one else who could help Lucy with this very specific problem, and Mrs. Gloucester was getting away!

Lucy sped down the two sets of stairs, skidding in her socks when she reached the bottom. Abigail had fallen asleep on the couch waiting for the girls to come down, which may have been the luckiest thing to happen to Lucy, ever. This was a matter that had to be handled immediately, and Lucy didn't have time to explain how her friend spontaneously disappeared into thin air. Lucy slinked past the couch and toward the front hall of the town house and grabbed her backpack. Opening the door as quickly and quietly as possible, Lucy hurtled down the front steps, watching Mrs. Gloucester start her car from across the street. She waved and flailed but Mrs. Gloucester didn't appear to notice her. As her car pulled out of the driveway, Lucy looked down at the ground in defeat. Now she'd never get Alyssa back, let alone in time for her flight to America.

Chapter Three

"Lucy, is everything all right?" Lucy jumped back, startled. Mrs. Gloucester was standing directly in front of her.

"Wait, I thought you were in your—," Lucy stammered.

"What's wrong?" Mrs. Gloucester gave her a concerned look. "I just realized I forgot to say goodbye to Mr. Poppins, and when I turned around there you were, looking like everything in the world was wrong."

Lucy sighed wth relief. "I've lost the golden loom, Mrs. Gloucester. My friend Alyssa took it and went into the portal to the magical world and I don't think she knows how to get back and who knows what could happen while she's there because there are ravines and crumbling castles and flying beasts and she doesn't have nearly as much experience looming as I do and she could be gone forev—"

"*Lucy* dear, slow down. I can't understand what you're trying to say."

"My friend Alyssa is supposed to go home today, but she took the loom and got transported through the bookcase to the magical world, and I don't know what to do."

"I see. I told you how important it was to keep the golden loom safe, Lucy. It's far more than a toy," said Mrs. Gloucester. "Come inside; I know just what we'll do."

Lucy followed Mrs. Gloucester into her town house across the street. Mr. Poppins was nuzzled in his bed in the living room, making loud snorting noises as he slept. Mrs. Gloucester brought Lucy to a closet near the kitchen. "Come along, dear," she said. They both entered the tiny closet, which barely fit the two of them. The smell of mothballs and old lady perfume filled Lucy's nostrils. Mrs. Gloucester was lost in the hanging jackets and Lucy couldn't tell what she was looking for. She started tapping on the wall. "Mrs. Gloucester, what are you doing?"

"Shh, this process can't be disrupted," she replied. Just when Lucy started to feel claustrophobic from standing in such tight quarters, Mrs. Gloucester mumbled, "Almost there." She tapped three more times on a low section of the wall of the closet. Lucy heard a series of grinding noises, like gears turning, and the light clinking of locks unlocking. Mrs. Gloucester moved further into the closet behind the coats so that Lucy couldn't see her anymore.

A moment passed, and Lucy realized that she was alone in the closet. "Mrs. Gloucester?" She squeezed herself through the coats on the hangers toward the wall, and, to her surprise, there was light shining from a small, window-shaped opening in the wall. Lucy craned her neck and peered inside. A big set of eyes was looking back at her and Lucy jumped.

"Well, are you coming?"

"I don't know how—how did you get in there? It's so small! I couldn't even fit an arm through there!"

"Don't be ridiculous, Lucy, it's just like any other door," Mrs. Gloucester said as she disappeared from sight.

Lucy leaned her head into the opening to get a better look and all of a sudden she was overcome by a dizzying sensation. She blinked, and was pulled into an elegant, colorful room where Mrs. Gloucester was shuffling through wooden drawers with funny looking knobs.

"What is this place?" Lucy asked. "This doesn't make sense. That closet is on the edge of your house! We should be in the garden by now!"

"It's another closet, just bigger. Like yours, this house came with some added features that can't be explained by traditional logic of the natural world," said Mrs. Gloucester. "I'm surprised you didn't realize that when you crossed over to the other realm!" She continued tinkering in a drawer until she looked satisfied. "Ah, here it is." From the depths of the drawer Lucy could hear something rattling. Mrs. Gloucester pulled out a shimmering Rainbow Loom hook. It glistened in the light, sending sparkles in every direction.

"Wow. That's beautiful!" Lucy gasped.

"It's the true pair to the golden loom. The glass hook you used before was only a placeholder. This hook and your magic loom are connected, Lucy. Do you see how it's twitching? It knows there's something wrong with the golden loom." Lucy looked on as the sparkly hook jumped about in Mrs. Gloucester's grasp. "Oh yes, and here are some extra elastics. Mrs. Gloucester handed Lucy a jar full of envelopes of elastics, as well as a bag to carry everything in. "Now, remember how I have a portal to the realm in my house, just like yours? You will need to use that one because Alyssa has already gone through yours. This will be a bit more complicated, because you don't have the magic loom to get you through. The hook will help, but it won't be enough. Do you have anything that belongs to Alyssa?"

Lucy lowered her head in disappointment; all of Alyssa's things were back at 163 Terrier Square. Then she had an idea. "I do! I have her friendship bracelet! It fell off her wrist in my room!" Lucy pulled the colorful band bracelet out of her pocket and handed it to Mrs. Gloucester, who examined it closely.

"This is very fine work. What I'll need to do is enchant the bracelet, which will allow it to become much like a key to the portal. This enchantment will only last a few seconds, so you won't have a moment to spare in crossing over. Can you do that?"

"I—I'll try," Lucy said, apprehensive.

"You will need to keep the bracelet and the hook on you *at all times*. If you lose them, you won't be able to get back." Lucy's heart was pounding. This was all very stressful. She nodded in agreement and Mrs. Gloucester went shuffling through more drawers. She pulled out several small multicolored vials. With a little rubber dropper, she dropped a tear's worth of liquid onto the bracelet from each bottle. The bracelet started to glow. "Okay, the portal is right here." Mrs. Gloucester pointed to the space right next to her, which, from Lucy's perspective, did not seem like anything other than thin air.

"Where?"

"Right here." Mrs. Gloucester grabbed Lucy's shoulders and moved her one pace to the right, just beneath an extravagant chandelier that glimmered above her. She handed Lucy the rubber band bracelet and the hook. The room started to quake, and the chandelier made loud jangling noises as it violently shook from the ceiling. Mrs. Gloucester said a series of words that Lucy couldn't quite make out, and then cried, "Now, Lucy! Jump!" Confused, Lucy didn't know where to go, but the hook had a will of its own and jerked her forward. Lucy felt the scene around her dissolve in a whirlwind.

"Mrs. Gloucester! Wait—I don't know how to find her!" But her words left her mouth without any sound, and then everything went dark.

Chapter Four

Lucy felt herself land on a hard, damp surface. She kept her eyes scrunched securely shut and took several deep breaths. The last thing she needed after a dizzying journey through realms was to puke everywhere. Slowly, she opened her eyes and looked around her at the familiar field of beautiful, colorful peonies that gave off the most delightful scent. In the distance, she could see the old swaying fir tree that held the passageway to her parents' bedroom. Beyond it was the dark forest and the tops of the turrets of the emerald castle. The old crumbling castle had been host to all sorts of adventures last year, and it was where she had met her friend Sallee.

Lucy took in the scenery, with the roving hills and the deep turquoise sky. Something was amiss. There were no birds or creatures, and there were large formations of upturned soil in the meadow of peonies. She walked through the field and inspected the destruction. Beside the piles of soil, there was green goo coming from car-sized divots. Lucy looked closely, just about to touch the green goo with her pointer finger, when a glob of it dripped onto a nearby peony. The peony made a loud popping noise and exploded, sending specks of goo and flower in every direction. A little landed on Lucy's shoe, which she shook off as fast as she could. Looking down, she could see her toe poking through the freshly burned hole in the top of her shoe.

"What happened here?" Lucy asked aloud to no one in particular. She followed the pathway of exploded goo through the meadow, carefully sidestepping pools of it as she went. In the distance, she saw a strange formation by the forest. She approached it slowly. It looked like it was shivering! As she got closer, she realized it was her zebra friends she had met the year prior—they were all cowering beneath the entrance to the forest! "Hi! What's going on, what are you all—"

"Shhh! You'll give us away!"

"I don't understand—what happened?" All at once the group of zebras snatched her into their circle.

"Hush! A witch has been here! She released the Horned Orogawg on us and destroyed our meadow!"

"What's a Horned Orogawg?" Lucy asked, confused.

"It's the most horrific monster in our land. It's as big as the tallest tree and fires exploding green goo from its jaws. The witch came through the fir tree and started meddling with our forest and agitating our friends. She sat and wove things with a loom, but everything she created just made our meadows worse! Her bands got stuck in the beaks of the birds and the webs she made clogged the river so that no more water would flow downstream. She tied knots into a rope that wrapped around the flowering Crotia trees and awoke the beast. Everyone knows that the pollen from the Crotia trees rouses the Horned Orogawg!"

This all sounded terrible, and Lucy could see that this beautiful magical place was in grave danger from all of the destruction. She saw that the river had begun to overflow into the meadow and drown the peonies. The water slowly crept inland, threatening the forest. Lucy also had an idea of who this witch was. "I don't think it was a witch at all," she told the animals. "I think it was my friend Alyssa. She hasn't been here before and she doesn't know how to use the magic loom! I need to find her so that I can stop her from doing any more damage."

"She went that way, toward the fuchsia castle." A zebra pointed her hoof in the direction of the goo-splattered divots.

"The fuchsia castle? I thought there was only the emerald castle," said Lucy.

"No, the emerald castle is in the Land of the Forest. The fuchsia castle is on the Volcan Trail."

"The *Volcan Trail*?" Lucy heard her voice go up an octave.

"It's the land beyond our forest and our meadows. The border terrain is rocky and volcanic, and anyone who goes there *probably* dies instantly. No one from our side who has crossed over has ever returned, so we made a pact long ago to stop venturing beyond our safe home."

"But what about Alyssa? Won't you help me find my friend? I don't know if I can go to the Volcan Trail by myself!" Lucy squeaked.

riverbank, and latched the ends of the barrier onto bordering trees.

Lucy went back into her sack and found a bag of bands labeled *Fishing*. Using her hook, she strung together dozens of these lime green bands, and attached a C-clip to the end. With all her might, she flung the end of the bands with the clip into the clogged river. With the barricade so close to the river's edge, the waters were beginning to rise, and Lucy did not have much time before it would be too deep for the zebras. She could feel the clip latch onto something in the river, and the elastics pulled tight. Her magical bands bounced back and revealed something stuck on the clip: a shoe.

But the water was still rising. She was running out of time. She wriggled the shoe off the line and tried again. This time, she felt another tug and again she pulled with all her might. The zebra leaned backward, struggling in the water to help Lucy bring the line in. At the end of the line was a massive wad of loom bands, which were heavy, sopping with water. Lucy readjusted her grip and flung the wad of bands from the end of the green line and back onto the meadow just as the water was reaching her chin. With the clump removed from the river, the water began to recede, and Lucy let out a relieved breath.

Lucy and all of the animals watched as the water began to flow down the river again and the meadow came back to life. The clog was gone, and the aquamarine barrier helped direct the river in its natural direction. Everyone cheered, "You did it, Lucy!"

Lucy was happy that she had made things better for her friends, but she knew she had to get going. "I'm going to go find my friend Alyssa, over on the Volcan Trail. I need to save her from the Horned Orogawg and bring her back home."

The animals all looked anxious at this, and one of the zebras warned her, "But *no one* returns from there! Your friend is gone; there's no way to save her."

"I don't believe that. Alyssa is here on her own and she is in danger. I *have* to save her. I just have to."

The two zebras looked at one another and seemed to communicate silently. They both nodded, and then one of them said gravely, "We appreciate that you have mended the wrongs your friend has done to us. We won't go with you, but if you call for us in a time of need, we will hear you and send help. Do not take this offer lightly, for it is only meant for a time of true desperation. Follow the craters that lead from the meadow—these are the footprints of the Horned Orogawg. They will lead you to the Volcan Trail and to the fuchsia castle. When you find the Horned Orogawg, you will find your friend."

Lucy nodded and hugged each of her animal friends. "Thank you. I'll see you again soon." The animals slowly retreated into the forest, and Lucy headed off in the direction of the goo-splattered Horned Orogawg footprints.

Chapter Five

Lucy trudged along the path, following the massive craters of upturned soil that led away from the beautiful meadows and roving hills. She sidestepped the green goo, which every so often seeped onto an unsuspecting crawler or flower, popped, and exploded, keeping Lucy alert. Taking in the massive size of the Horned Orogawg footprints sent chills up Lucy's spine. It was certain to be a giant beast, and Lucy did not know if she had the skills or resources to outwit something so daunting. As she traipsed along, the ground became more desolate, shifting from kaleidoscopic pastures and vegetation, to dusty lands sparsely decorated with dying plants.

Off in the distance, she saw dark cloud formations along the base of a mountain range. When she arrived at the base, it was covered with ashen soil and charred shrubbery. She looked up, and high at the top of the mountain she saw the bright red-orange glow—flowing lava. Lucy had never seen a volcano in real life before, and there seemed to be hundreds of them that extended far beyond this one, like a natural border.

She looked around, realizing that the Horned Orogawg's footprints had stopped. If she couldn't find the Horned Orogawg, she would never be able to find Alyssa! She scoured the base of the volcano in search of a clue. As she made her way around the scorched rocks, she saw that there was something different about one part of the volcano. She climbed over a boulder, and was surprised to see a cave entrance. The entrance was the size of a ship, and she couldn't believe she hadn't seen it earlier. She thought that there must have been some sort of enchantment along the cave opening that kept it hidden from far away.

Lucy climbed down into the cave entrance and took in her surroundings. It was dark, smelled of putrid sulfur, and an acidic liquid dripped from the ceiling walls, sizzling as it made its way to the cave floor.

As soon as Lucy's eyes adjusted to the darkness, she realized what a horrific mistake she had made. Towering in front of her was the Horned Orogawg, seated squarely in front of what looked like a door. The Horned Orogawg was gargantuan, with greenish-black prismatic scales that flickered ribbons of dark purple light. His head was covered in horns the color of onyx, his teeth a sharp, bright orange, and his eyes as indigo as the darkest depths of the ocean.

Lucy quivered and took a deep breath. The Horned Orogawg snarled and snapped his razor teeth back at her. She held her breath, standing where she was like a tree trunk so as not to provoke the monster. Slowly, she pulled a small collection of bands from out of her bag, labeled *Distraction*.

Swiftly and quietly, she looped band after band onto her hook while the Horned Orogawg glared at her. One of the bands snapped, and the Horned Orogawg shot a fiery ball of green goo at her. She hopped and it missed her by an inch. She continued looping, until she had what she needed. She tossed her rubber band creation into the air, and it shot up to the top of the cave. Its bands were the prettiest colors Lucy had ever seen, but she was unsure what to expect. She hadn't made it with anything in particular in mind, just an earnestness to get out of this cave and away from the beast.

The Horned Orogawg bolted upright, following the trajectory of the rising form. He held it in his gaze and shot a new clump of green goo at it. Lucy covered her ears and hid behind a stalagmite, waiting for the popping sound and inevitable explosion. But the sound and burst never came. She peered out from behind the sharp rock structure and saw that the Horned Orogawg was transfixed with a hovering orb. She looked more carefully and saw that the orb was actually a beautiful butterfly, surrounded by a bright protective field covered in the goo. The butterfly glimmered against the shimmering reflections of the Horned Orogawg's scales. The Horned Orogawg calmed, transfixed by the floating creature. Lucy looked past the Horned Orogawg and saw that there was a clear path to the door behind the monster.

Quickly, she pulled out a glass jar from her bag and used a rock to scoop some of the Horned Orogawg's green goo into the jar.

Lucy closed the lid and ran along the cave wall to get to the door. The door was old, with an ornate iron handle that clicked loudly when she opened it. Taking one last look back at the Horned Orogawg, which was still staring peacefully at the colorful butterfly, Lucy passed through the door.

❀ ❀ ❀

Lucy entered a dark hallway in the depths of the volcano. She was enveloped in heat and steam and was disoriented by the darkness. She rustled through her bag and found the *Torch* bands. Fashioning them together using her hook, she created what looked like an old-fashioned fiery torch from the enchanted glowing bands. Light cast in every direction, and Lucy could now see down the rocky path. Moisture dripped from the volcanic walls and pebbles crunched under Lucy's feet as she trekked down the winding corridor.

She walked for what seemed like an eternity with no sign of an exit. Just as Lucy began to get very anxious, worrying that perhaps there was no way out, she rounded a corner and saw a hazy glow in the distance. As she got closer, she came upon a golden door ahead of her that glistened in the darkness of the passageway. The door handle was made of fire opal, with turquoise and orange flecks glittering against the gold of the passage. Lucy grasped the handle, which warmed to the touch. With all her strength, she pulled the heavy door open and was met with blinding light.

Chapter Six

Lucy's eyes adjusted to the bright light as she exited the cavernous volcano. She gasped—before her was a scene she never could have imagined. The landscape shone with bright turquoise skies, lavender clouds, and fields of fruit trees. In the distance, a beautiful mountain range with swirling peaks, rocky formations that looked like elaborate drip castles made of sand, and a clear lake the color of jade. And right before her was a pristine castle made of glittering *fuchsia* crystal. "The fuchsia castle!" Lucy shouted victoriously. This was not what Lucy had expected. She had imagined the castle to be on the Volcan Trail, not someplace so beautiful. Her friends in the Land of the Forest had made it sound like the Volcan Trail would last forever—maybe they didn't know how lovely it was here!

Lucy walked around the perimeter of the castle, trying to find clues for where Alyssa may have gone. Lucy walked through the gardens, which had the most incredible flowers that she had ever seen—some purred quiet songs, others twirled and danced, and some spit sparks in a rainbow of colors.

As she found her way to the back of the castle, Lucy looked up in awe. There stood the tallest tower she had ever seen. It was made of shimmering, diamond-shaped magenta glass, with intricate designs scattered up the length of the tower. The base was lined with a fence and lovely blue flowers.

Lucy stared at the mesmerizing crystal, wondering where such glass could come from, when she thought she felt something hit her head. She looked around and saw nothing and no one. A moment later, she felt another light tap. She spun around, looking for the culprit, and found no one still. All of a sudden, something rained down on her, pelting her on the head and shoulders. She looked at the ground to see dozens of bright blue rubber bands! She looked up, and at the peak of the crystal tower she saw a beautiful princess waving from above.

"Lucy! Lucy, I'm up here!" Shouted a familiar voice. It wasn't a princess at all—it was Alyssa!

"Alyssa! I found you! I'm so happy to see you!"

"Lucy, I'm so sorry for taking your magic loom," Alyssa shouted from up high in the tower. "I just really wanted to see what you had been talking about. I wanted to see the emerald castle and to meet all your friends. It all sounded so wonderful and enchanting, and I thought I knew enough about looming that I could figure everything out by myself. But I was wrong. I feel so terrible. There was a horrific monster that nearly ate me and it made a mess of the meadow. The only reason I got past it was because I used the last of the invisibility bands and snuck away. I understand if you think I'm a bad friend. I deserve it."

"It's okay, Alyssa. I knew where you had gone right away and I think I would have done the same thing. Everything in the Land of the Forest is fine now; I figured out how to fix the meadow, so don't worry! But why are we shouting? Let me up there!"

"I—I can't," Alyssa answered solemnly.

"What do you mean you *can't*? Where's the door? I'll just come up. I bet the view is amazing!"

"No, Lucy, I'm stuck up here. There's no door. I got through the volcano and was wandering around the castle. I lay down in the garden because I was tired and when I woke up, I was locked up here. It's not all that awful, actually. There are lots of books to read and games to play, and food appears on the table when I get hungry. But I miss you and I miss my family. I just want to go home to America now."

"Okay . . . so you're locked in a tower but you're not being starved or married off to some evil prince or anything?"

"Nope. I just kind of hang out. The library is pretty extensive, so I've been reading. And I found a regular Rainbow Loom to use so that I don't accidentally destroy things anymore."

"So, er, do you want to stay?"

"*No!* I mean, sure, it's fine as far as being imprisoned goes but I'm still imprisoned!" Alyssa started to sound desperate.

Lucy would have to think of something. She studied the tower and noticed that there were silver spikes placed periodically up the height of the fortress. They would be perfect to climb up. Lucy put a steady foot onto the gate that separated her from the blue flowers and the tower. She pulled herself up, with two feet balanced on the gate and her hands leaning against the crystal turret. Lucy edged to the closest set of spikes, and began to put one foot on it to steady herself. She put all of her weight onto the spike, but suddenly, the spike pulled back violently, disappearing into the crystal tower, and Lucy lost her footing. She grabbed onto another spike, which made her hand itch uncontrollably.

Beneath her, the blue flowers began to bloom, shooting out hissing steam that made Lucy very dizzy. Losing her grip, she fell back over the fence and stumbled onto the grass. Catching her breath, Lucy realized that this would not be as easy as she had hoped.

"Lucy! Are you all right?" Alyssa called down with worry from the tower window.

"Yeah, I think so," Lucy groaned, "Okay, I'm going to use the bands to make something to come and get you. Can you throw down the golden loom? The hook takes too long on its own."

"Heads up!" Alyssa tossed down the golden loom and Lucy caught it. Now holding both the magic loom and the sparkling hook, Lucy watched them glow and hum with delight. She could tell the matching set would do powerful things when used together. Lucy looked up at the tower and took a minute to decide what to do next. She rifled through her bag and found a bag of bands labeled *Storm*. No, that wouldn't do. She found another that read *Catapult*. Catapulting could work, but it was risky and imprecise. Finally, Lucy nodded when she found a bag that was labeled *Suction*.

"Perfect. Alyssa, give me a second and I'll figure something out!" Using the golden loom and the glimmering hook, Lucy worked with supernatural speed. Soon she had two matching suction cups the size of her hands. Using a fishtail stitch, she wove straps to complete the paddles. She tried them on, making sure they fit tightly around her hands. Lucy hopped back onto the fence, leaning her hands against the glass. Lucy had always been strong for her size, but she knew this would test her abilities more than she was used to.

Taking a deep breath, she removed one suction cup from the glass to reach higher on the tower. There was a loud suction noise, and a smack when it hit back on the glass. Below her, the vicious blue blossoms started to open up again. Working as quickly as she could, Lucy used all of her strength to move up the crystal tower, hearing the suction and smacking each time she moved up.

Halfway there, Lucy began to grow tired. Her arm muscles ached, and her hands were starting to sweat. She looked down beneath her, and realized just how high up she was. Lucy had never been afraid of heights, but she had also never scaled a magical fortress before. The highest she had ever been was on the London Eye, and that was basically a very fancy Ferris wheel. The land below looked miniscule. If she fell, she would be a goner. She felt her hands start to slip from the sweat. She squinted up at Alyssa, who had a worried look on her face. "Come on, Lucy. You can do it. You're almost here!" Alyssa cheered.

The encouragement helped. Lucy mustered up all her might and continued up the tower. She was just a few arms' lengths away when the crystal tower started to rattle. The shaking grew so forceful that Lucy lost her grip on one of the suction cups and was dangling from one arm. Then she saw it: a giant, spider-like monster was racing straight for her. And this was no ordinary spider. It looked like some sort of military-grade robot, with sharp legs that clacked against the glass and laser-red eyes that scoped her out. Lucy screamed as the spider shot its web at her once, twice, a dozen times. Soon she was trapped in the spider's sticky netting against the crystal. "*Lucy!*" wailed Alyssa, who was just out of reach to help her.

The spider retreated, returning to wherever it had come from. But Lucy was stuck. The web pressed against her skin, growing tighter, and Lucy became short of breath. This was too much. The web was so tight that she couldn't reach her golden loom in her bag. She tried to tear at the netting, but it was too strong. "Alyssa, I'm stuck! I don't know what to do! I can't breathe!" She could hear Alyssa at the window, frantic and beginning to cry.

Suddenly, a loud wind picked up. Lucy peered through the web and saw bright green eyes staring back at her. It was a man in a cerulean cloak, with a graying beard and a lined and serious face. He was hovering in a bronze chariot in the shape of a winged horse. The wings flapped heavily, and the man waved his hand across the web, which slowly released Lucy as he held on to her. He pulled her into the chariot, and Lucy stumbled onto the indigo velvet seats. "My friend Alyssa is up there! Please help her, too! She's been captured!" The man met her eyes with a stern look for just a moment, and then he turned his gaze up and saw Alyssa. A look of horror came across his face. He steered the chariot to Alyssa's window, and she climbed out onto the seat next to Lucy.

Without a word, the man flew the chariot to a flat roof of the castle. He climbed out of the chariot, and raised steady hands up to help Lucy and Alyssa hop down. He looked down at them somberly, and after a few moments he said, "It's okay. Come in for tea." The man turned on his heel and headed toward the understated entrance, his cloak whipping in the wind. Lucy and Alyssa followed closely behind.

Chapter Seven

Lucy grasped Alyssa's hand as they walked through the doorway and into the castle. She was happy to have her friend back, but the man was walking quickly down the hallway and there was no time for celebration. At the end of the hallway, they met a grand staircase. The man seemed to glide in his cerulean cloak as he made his way down. Lucy grasped the railing as she made her first step down the staircase, and it took hold of her. The staircase worked like an escalator, and Lucy didn't need to do anything but hold on. She turned back to Alyssa, who smiled and followed suit. The two girls soared down the palatial winding staircase and came to a smooth halt at the bottom. They followed the man in the cloak into a smaller room, which was decorated in beautiful abstract art, filled with vivid colors and texture. The fuchsia glass glittered along the walls, painting the wandering fields behind the castle a lovely pink.

The man gestured for them to sit down, and the two girls curled up close to each other on a comfy, pillowy couch. Tea and biscuits appeared on the metallic coffee table. The plate was filled with all of Lucy's favorite chocolate biscuits and even the coconut ones that Alyssa liked. The china kettle was steaming hot. The man poured tea for both of them. Then he poured some for himself, and the three sat in silence for several minutes as they drank the sweet tea.

Lucy broke the heavy silence. "So . . ."

The man looked up, waiting for her to continue.

"Well, um, I'm a little confused. You saved us from the tower, but then you brought us into the castle, which means that the tower is also yours. I don't mean to be rude, but I think this means you kidnapped my friend, booby-trapped the tower, and set a murderous spider loose on me. Right?" she said, looking to Alyssa for agreement. Alyssa clearly had not made this connection yet, and her mouth gaped open. "I guess what I am hoping is that having tea is not just an interlude to a much more devious kidnapping plot."

"Lucy!" Alyssa hissed.

The man rubbed his brow and laughed, but the sadness did not leave his eyes. "You're a clever girl—" He paused.

"Lucy. And this is Alyssa."

"Lucy," He nodded at both of them. "I fear I have made a terrible mistake. And for that, I apologize." After a moment, Lucy raised an eyebrow. She would need a better explanation than that. The man sighed and scratched his beard. "You see, I once had a daughter, named Elana, and she was about your age. We had a terrible argument, because she wanted to cross the Volcan Trail, travel to the Land of the Forest, and see the emerald castle. I told her it was too dangerous, and Elana told me she was bored here and wanted to see the realm. She was my only child, and the Land of the Forest is a treacherous place. All those who have made the journey have never returned. I did not want that for her, and would not go either. I have a kingdom to care for."

Lucy remembered that the zebra had said just the same thing about this side of the Volcan

Trail, and she had been wrong. Both places thought the other was deadly and it wasn't true! She bit her tongue, though, allowing the king to finish his story.

"So, one morning, she never came out from her room. I went to check on her, and she was gone. She had run away, and left me no way to reach her. I was heartbroken. But then when I found your friend here sleeping in the garden, I thought my daughter had returned," he paused, before looking Alyssa and smiling sadly, "You look *just* like her. You have the same gold hair, and there aren't very many little girls around the castle. I was afraid you would leave again, so I put you in the locked tower until I could figure out what to say. I am so sorry if I frightened you."

"Phew! I thought you were going to keep us here forever!" chimed in Lucy. Alyssa gave her a frantic look. Lucy continued, "I'm sorry. That's a very sad story, and I'm glad we cleared up all this confusion. But I think we should be on our way now. I hope you find your daughter, really." She began to stand up from her seat on the couch.

Alyssa kicked Lucy's leg, forcing her back down on the couch. The man shook his head at them and said, "I'm sorry, but I'm going to insist that you stay. It's much too dangerous out there. You can have the whole castle to yourselves and there is everything you could want right here. I lost one daughter once, and I refuse to do it again." He stood up and began to walk out of the room.

"*Wait!*" cried Lucy. The king turned. "Well, the thing is, we're *not* your daughters. We have our own parents in London and America."

The king gave her a blank look and said, "Is that beyond the emerald castle?"

"Er, yes. Much, *much* further beyond," replied Lucy.

"I understand, but you are not going to convince me. You will learn to enjoy it here. You may choose rooms upstairs; there are hundreds." He began to turn again.

Lucy ran up to him and pulled on his cloak to stop him. "Please! How about—"

"There's nothing you can say," the king interjected.

"But there is!" Lucy pulled out her magic loom and her sparkling hook. The king looked at them, puzzled. "I have a magic loom. I can do anything with it. I bet I can even find your daughter. I came from the Land of the Forest, crossed the Volcan Trail, and outwitted the Horned Orogawg!"

The king's eyebrows lifted. "You got past the Horned Orogawg?"

Lucy nodded and continued, "I used a distraction charm I created with my hook. I even got most of the way up the tower before the demon spider attacked me!"

"That's true. How would you find her?"

"I know there's a way. I have friends who could help me if necessary. I promise Alyssa and I can help!"

"Okay, but not Alyssa. Just you. I cannot risk both of you. I will allow you to go and she can stay here. You can go to my supply room and take what you need for your journey."

Lucy sighed in relief and held out her hand. She could handle this. "Deal."

Chapter Eight

The king had shown Lucy to the supply room, where she had expected to find things like hiking gear and tools. Instead, the shelves were filled with every kind of magic loom rubber band she could ever dream of. Not having much time, she chose envelopes at random, hoping they would be of use to her later on.

"Elana would not have gone through the back volcano entrance. You will need to go the long way through the valley, across the fields, through the forest, through the kingdom gates, and over the mountain range, if she made it that far." Lucy nodded and began walking down the stone steps of the fuchsia castle. "Oh, and Lucy," said the graying king, "she likes fire blossoms."

Lucy nodded and waved back to both the king and Alyssa as she began her journey. She walked down the winding path of the great castle, taking in the scenery as she went. She knew very little about Elana, but it seemed they shared a curiosity for new things. Hadn't Lucy herself wanted something more exciting than her dull life at 163 Terrier Square? She had been drawn to the possibilities that the magic loom could offer her. Maybe Elana felt the same way about exploring the unknown.

Lucy wandered through the valley, hoping she was going in the right direction. Instead of meadows of peonies, there were strange flowers that looked like pinwheels. She picked one up and spun it. Suddenly, all of the pinwheels in the meadow began to spin, faster and faster. The wind picked up, and Lucy watched as the field began to whir, building wild, swirling winds. The peaceful lavender clouds above her turned to a dark violet, and funnel clouds formed over the meadow. Twisters! Lucy didn't know what to do. There was a copper-colored bush nearby, and she crawled over to it on the side against the wind and held onto it tightly. In the small bit of relief she had under the bush, whose bright copper leaves were quickly flying off their branches, Lucy searched through her bag of supplies for some help. She tossed through bands that read *Cotton Candy*, *Bubbles*, and *Quicksand*. None of those would help. With the wind whipping at her face, Lucy finally came across an envelope that was labeled *Cape*.

Thankful for her magic loom and its sparkling hook, Lucy strung hundreds of crimson magic bands together in a flash. She had loomed an amazing cape, perhaps even better than that of the most powerful superhero. She tied the ends of the cape around her neck, letting the rest of it flow impressively behind her.

Standing up from beneath the protective shrub, Lucy darted into the wind. She soared up and up and up, dodging the pinwheel flowers that had flown into the air as sharply as spinning buzz saws. Up high, the violet twisters looked like dancers floating across a grand stage. With the wind under her cape, Lucy rose above to the calm lavender clouds and breathed in the fresh air.

She passed out of the danger of the meadow, but as she was heading toward the ground, a stray pinwheel flower flung past her. Suddenly, she felt like she wasn't floating anymore. She was falling! The pinwheel had sliced across her amazing cape! Lucy was in a nosedive, headed for the ground.

As quickly as she could, she pulled out her magic loom and grabbed the first bag: *Cotton Candy*. She flung the bands together on the loom, coming closer and closer to the ground with each looping and hooking motion. In desperation, Lucy released the cotton candy from the loom, hurtling into the ground with a great thud.

Lucy was facedown, blissfully aware that she was okay. She opened her mouth to breathe, and instead she tasted the sweetest and most delightful sugar. Pushing herself up with her hands, Lucy rose from the bed of cotton candy. It had saved her! Winded and relieved, Lucy sat for a minute eating pieces of her cotton candy before she had to get back up.

She sat up and dusted herself off. Turning around to look at the destruction behind her, Lucy watched as the violet funnel clouds dissolved back into the sky and the pinwheel meadow settled down. The clouds returned to their swirling lavender color, as if no disturbance had been made at all.

Lucy continued on her trek, heading into the beginning of the fruit crops. The trees were a bizarre shape that Lucy had never seen before, with geometric branches and neon fruit. The fruits were different on each tree. She found a pear tree and snapped a ripe pear off a branch. It smelled okay, so she bit into it. And immediately spit it out. It tasted vile! She threw the pear onto the ground in disgust. She went to the next tree, which had oranges. She peeled an orange, and out squirted a bright blue acid that smelled of rotten eggs. "Ew!" She dropped the orange, splattering blue liquid at the base of the tree. The grass shriveled up and turned a rotting brown color.

Trying once more, Lucy went to the next tree with unfamiliar-looking fruit. It was teal in color with jutting edges and small prickles coming out from the skin. It didn't look particularly appetizing, but Lucy tried to pry it open. It wouldn't budge, so she took out her sparkling hook and stabbed the fruit with the hook end, sending the hook into the center of the fruit. The fruit opened wide, and exposed bright purple juicy seeds. This time fruit smelled wonderful. Lucy took a seat under the tree and began eating the delicious fruit.

As she scraped the inside of the fruit clean, Lucy began to drift off in thought. *What a beautiful place. Why would Elana ever want to leave here?*

Because I wanted to see the realm.

Where would she go, this mysterious golden haired princess who looked so much like Alyssa?

Where the earth meets the sky and water flows up.

I wish I knew how to find her. I wonder if she really hated her kingdom so much. Her father didn't seem all that bad. He just wanted to protect her, after all. It would be better if he weren't holding Alyssa hostage, though.

He'll let her go if you find me. I want to come home now.

Lucy bolted up from her comfortable position against the tree. Was she hearing what she thought she was hearing?

Yes.

Who is this?

Elana. You just ate a parapet. They have telepathic qualities. One fruit won't be enough, though; its power will wear out.

What? How?

It's not important, just come and get me. I'm stuck.

But where are you, Elana?

I told you. Where the earth meets the sky and water flows up. I can't reach you. Find your way through the mountain range, and cross the—

Elana! Cross the what?

Elana's voice faded out, and Lucy couldn't hear where she was supposed to go. She climbed the parapet tree, searching for more fruit to reconnect with Elana. But it was useless; the tree had been picked off, and Lucy had eaten the last one. She slumped down to the ground in defeat. She was so close to learning where to find Elana.

Standing up, Lucy trudged through the fruit groves in disappointment and frustration. Right now, she was desperate to know how to get to Elana. "Where the sun meets the sky" could be anywhere! It was the least helpful clue that Lucy could possibly think of. While she did not want to burden her friends from the Land of the Forest, she knew that her only choice right now as to ask them for help. The zebras had said that she could ask for help if she were desperate, and now was definitely that time. After all, this side of the Volcan Trail was not nearly as bad as all of the animals had made it out to be. Maybe if she could show the animals on the other side how lovely this side of the realm was, they could all live in harmony and not be so afraid of one another. It all really just boiled down to a giant misunderstanding.

Lucy looked through her bag, searching for what she needed. Finally, she found the *Flare* rubber bands. Using her hook and her loom, she knew that this message needed to be perfect. If it weren't powerful enough to travel back to the Land of the Forest and find her friends, she might be stuck here forever. She sat down and pulled out her golden loom and her sparkling hook. They felt right in her hands, as if she were the only person in the world who could use them well and to do good things.

She strung band after band together, pulling and looping the magic bands up and down the magic loom. At one point, a band snapped and she had to start all over. This time, she decided to use two bands at once. The flare needed to be sturdy and powerful, and she couldn't risk having the message break mid-flight.

Taking two of each of the powerful bands, she wrapped them around the pegs and made a pattern on the loom. When she got to the bottom of the loom, she wrapped another band tightly on the very last peg to secure it. Using her sparkling hook, she pulled the bands on the bottom peg up and through the opening, and began to loop the bands back to secure them. The magic bands looked like rain drops along her golden loom, which was actually quite pretty. When she had looped all of the rubber bands, she secured the formation with a final knot of another magic band. Slowly and carefully, she pulled it off of her loom.

She gasped. It was perfect. Lucy held the flare out in front of her and tossed it into the sky. The flare went up and up and up. It blazed against the turquoise sky and lavender clouds, leaving a trail of sparkling dust in its wake. She watched it travel back across the fields, over the pinwheel meadows, around the crystal castle, and over the tops of the dark, steaming volcanoes. The flare's bright changing colors faded against the horizon as it went out of sight.

Giddy at watching the power of the creation she had made, Lucy felt accomplished. She knew she would not hear back for a while, if at all, so she would have to keep moving forward in the meantime. She crossed her fingers, hoping that her friends in the Land of the Forest would recognize the message and be able to help. If she did not hear from them, Lucy was unsure how she would get by. But if she had to do it by herself, at least she knew she had tried everything. Smiling and feeling reenergized, Lucy headed out of the fruit groves and reached the gates of the kingdom.

Chapter Nine

Looking up at the beautiful gates, Lucy took one last look back at the kingdom. She knew her journey would be difficult, but she was glad that she knew just how lovely this place was, and not the horrific danger zone that her friends in the Land of the Forest had thought it would be. She passed through the gates, and scoped out her options when she arrived at the bottom of the mountain range. There was a massive cliff face, with shimmering rocks that looked too slippery to climb. She watched as rocks skidded off the side and soared to the bottom, obliterating into sand as soon as they hit the ground. Today was not the day to learn how to rock climb. Next to the cliff were two winding paths. One seemed to go straight up to the peak of the mountain, and the other one meandered. While the straight line would certainly get her up the mountain faster, Lucy wasn't even sure if that was how Elana would have gone. And it was too steep, so she started for the direction of the meandering path.

Shortly after she began hiking, Lucy's legs started to burn and she was quickly out of breath. Even though she had chosen the longer path, it was still pretty steep and rocky. Along the way, she passed trees that changed colors and shapes of their bark like turning kaleidoscopes. As she passed one of them, a colorful branch fell to the ground. Lucy knelt down and examined it. It certainly didn't look like it was going to attack or poison her. She held on to it and kept moving.

She trudged on, growing more weary as she climbed. The trees were a nice distraction, but not distracting enough to keep her from thinking about how much her legs were burning. She looked down at the branch she was holding, and noticed that sap was coming out of a crack in the branch. It was a bright metallic blue, and dripped on her hands. It was cool to the touch at first, but then suddenly her whole arm was warm and the scrapes she had from the pinwheels had disappeared She wondered if this were because of the sap, or if she had just imagined it. To test it out, she dropped a little dab of the sap onto the hole that the Horned Orogawg's green goo had singed into her shoe. The hole closed up, and the blister on her toe didn't hurt anymore! Feeling more adventurous, Lucy dabbed more sap along her arms, face, and legs. She was filled with chills, followed by a comforting warmth. She felt like she could run a marathon!

Lucy began to run up the trail, hopping over rocks and around trees. She was so excited about her newfound energy that she did not notice that she was being followed. As she skipped along, a crowd of small creatures began to form around her. Had she been paying attention, she would have noticed their sharp teeth, their beady eyes, and the grumbling of their hungry stomachs. They had mean faces, sharp, prickly fur that stood on end, and claws that glowed red-hot like a fireplace poker.

Lucy skipped along until she came upon a fallen tree. But this was no ordinary tree. It was the length of a football field and two stories high. She was going to have to figure out how to either get around or over it. As she stood there, considering, she heard the grinding of gravel and the snapping of branches. She froze, knowing that there was someone behind her. She pivoted around, and came face to face with what seemed like hundreds of sinister deer-sized creatures. She couldn't put a name to them, but she knew they were dangerous and were not planning on letting her escape over the tree. Slowly, they inched forward, baring their terrifying jaws.

Lucy tried to remain calm and think about how she could get out of her situation. Slowly, still watching the creatures, she reached into her bag and pulled out her loom and some bands. She started looming, not knowing what she was doing and hoping the bands would be useful to her. She looked down at what she had created, and her expression turned from panic to a wide grin. She had made a slingshot with a place to hold something to shoot.

Digging into her bag again, she couldn't find any marbles or things to shoot from the slingshot. She looked at the ground and saw rocks, but they were all well out of distance, and reaching for them would give the animals the opportunity to lunge for her. She considered the contents of her bag a second time, and this time she noticed the jar of the Horned Orogawg's green goo. Using her hook, she scooped the goo into the basket of the slingshot.

Taking a deep breath, she made eye contact with the leader of the animal pack. He gritted his teeth at her and barked ferociously. Not missing her chance, Lucy flung her first shot of green goo in the space right in front of the leader. The green goo exploded, and the creature fled.

Lucy rejoiced! She had stopped him! But her face fell as she realized that she had to deal with all of the others. In the confusion of what happened to their leader, the monsters began barking at one another trying to figure out what to do. Lucy took this opportunity to fling more green goo in their direction. This was good, but it would not be enough to ward off all of the animals in such a large group.

The creatures that remained snapped at her and began to charge. Lucy shrieked and started to climb the branches of the tree, getting just out of reach of the animals. She hoisted herself onto a limb, and grabbed her loom from her bag. She found the *Quicksand* bands and began looping away with her loom. As soon as she was finished, she tossed the quicksand onto the ground below, where the angry beasts were jumping just beneath her. As the ground began to move, the creatures slowly backed away.

Lucy did not know how long the quicksand would last, so she turned and climbed up the wall of branches on the massive tree trunk. She climbed and climbed, scuffing her hands and sweating as she soldiered on. After what seemed like forever, Lucy reached the top of the tree. She looked down, and the animals seemed to have drifted off. Only a few still remained, and they were no longer paying any attention to her. She waited a few minutes longer and then quietly lowered herself carefully down and ran off as quickly as she could.

Chapter Ten

As Lucy dusted herself off from all the commotion from before, she took a look around her. To her surprise, she wasn't all that far from the peak of the mountain! She picked up her pace and hiked the rest of the way, being careful to pay attention to her surroundings so that she knew she was not being followed or in any danger. As she approached the summit, Lucy grew anxious. What if she had come all this way and then discovered that there was nothing on the other side of the mountain? She reached the peak, and saw that the snowcapped mountaintop looked like it was connected to the sky.

Wait! Lucy thought, excitedly. *Where the earth meets the sky! It's here!* Lucy thought for a moment and tried to remember the rest of Elana's clue. She scanned the skyline and looked around her. It was stunning. The sky shone a brilliant turquoise, and the only clouds in sight were small wisps of lavender fog in the valley below. Far across from her was another mountain peak the same height as hers. And in between was a magnificent stream of shooting water. Alyssa had told her about visiting Old Faithful in America. *A geyser!* Lucy stared at it in awe, watching the water flow upward as high as the mountaintops. *Where the earth meets the sky and the water flows up.* This was it!

For a moment, Lucy felt triumphant. She had figured out the clue, traveled great distances, and fought off scary creatures to find Elana. And then it occurred to her: *Where was Elana?* This area was so vast, with two mountain peaks and a giant geyser in the middle. She could be anywhere! Lucy threw her bag down and sat against a rock. With her chin resting against her hands, she tried to think hard about what to do next. It was all so daunting, but she was determined. She had promised she would bring Elana home, no matter what.

Off in the distance, Lucy heard a flapping sound. She looked up, and fast approaching was an elegant black bird, soaring right for her. In its mouth, the bird had an ivory box. The bird flew over Lucy, pausing just long enough to drop the box at her feet, and then flew off again. Lucy approached the rectangular box and picked it up carefully. She opened it and gasped. It was a silver loom! It came with a sparkling hook, just like the one she had! What would she do with two magic looms, though? Engraved inside the box, it read HELP WHEN IT IS NEEDED. Lucy was so excited that she hugged the box. Her friends from the Land of the Forest had come through for her!

She pondered for a moment, realizing that this loom needed to reach Elana. If she could send it off to her, then Elana could use the bands to create wings or a rocket or some sort of amazing contraption that would get her closer to Lucy. Lucy looked back in the box, and underneath where the silver loom rested were two bags that read *Bridge Side 1* and *Bridge Side 2*. It was all becoming clear. If she could just get this loom and one of the bags to Elana, then they could meet each other halfway! Lucy scoured through her bag and realized she was running low on bands. What could possibly help her in this situation? None of these bands had radar or special locators to find a missing person. The task seemed impossible. All she had left were *Parachutes*, *Skis*, and *Bubbles*.

"Bubbles!" shouted Lucy. She snatched up her loom and hook and began looping away with the *Bubble* bands. Her bubble grew and grew, until it was big enough to hold the ivory box with the magic loom and hook inside. She gently placed the magic set into the bubble, and pushed it off into the air. She whispered, "Go to Elana!" and the bubble floated quickly away from the peak. Lucy watched it go, hoping that this would work and she was not just sending a perfectly good magic loom off to who knows where. The bubble glided across the valley, went around the geyser, and soared to the other peak.

Lucy waited, knowing that this might take a while. She sat on the mountaintop patiently, trying to stay focused in case anything happened. Just as she started to drift off in a daydream, she saw a flicker of light. Lucy jumped up, waiting to see if the light came again. From across the valley and over the massive waterspout, another silver flicker of light glinted against the mountain backdrop. Lucy grabbed her golden loom and held it against the sky, turning it to reflect light across the valley. The silver light returned. It was Elana!

Now that they both had a loom, Lucy pulled out her bag of bands for the bridge. The magic bands were dazzling gold, with flecks of dark pink gems and diamond throughout. She attached the bands to her loom, making sure to use two on each peg so that the bridge would not break. There would be nothing worse than getting partway across and having it collapse. She arranged the bands with incredible speed and accuracy, and looped them back with her hook with even greater skill. She had really become a loom expert.

The bridge began to form, and Lucy secured the base to the edge of the peak. She continued working away, building the bridge out from the mountain and over the plummeting valley below. The bridge hung in midair with strength and structure that only the magic bands could provide. Lucy was careful not to look anywhere but the section she was working on. She couldn't risk getting dizzy and falling off.

She worked away, creating a beautiful suspension bridge that was beginning to arch above where the geyser would be. As she approached the beautiful, natural waterspout, she looked up to see the spray of the water creating rainbows against streams of light. It was lovely.

Just beyond it, she could see the formation of the other half of the bridge. This one was brilliant silver, with flecks diamond and emerald scattered about. She could see a flicker of gold hair at the end of the other structure, and was excited to finally meet Elana.

Both Lucy and Elana were just paces away from connecting their sections of bridge. They worked quickly and skillfully, and Lucy was impressed at how quickly Elana was able to use the magic loom. It was as if she had been doing it for years! They were just above the geyser, and only an arm's length away from connecting the gold and silver sections of the bridge. The spray from the water was misting onto the bridge. As Lucy reached with her loom to add more to the structure, she slipped on the slick bridge and lost her footing. She screamed and the fall tossed her over the side of the ledge. She grasped onto the edge with one hand.

"Elana, help!"

The golden haired princess jumped down onto her stomach on the ledge of the silver side of the bridge, and reached out. "Grab my hand!"

"No! You have to finish your side or I won't be able to get up!" Lucy shouted back, her feet getting soaked from the spray of water coming from beneath her. She was having a hard time holding on, and she needed Elana to hurry so she could get leverage on both sides. Elana worked faster than Lucy had ever been able to work with her magic loom, and suddenly the silver side was complete. Elana leaned over, this time much closer to Lucy, and grabbed her by the shoulders. She had strapped herself to the bridge using extra magic bands to make sure she was secure when pulling Lucy up.

Together, they used all of their strength to get Lucy up onto the ledge and away from the shooting water. Panting, Lucy rolled back onto the gold side of the bridge, wiping the wet hair off of her face. She sat back up, and saw a grinning Elana directly across from her on the silver side. "Come on! Your turn to finish!"

Exhausted and with her hands shaking, Lucy began the last bit of the golden bridge. "Last one together?" Lucy held up the final bands to Elana.

"You got it!" Elana replied, and the two of them secured the golden and silver band in the crossing between the two colossal mountain peaks. They both jumped up and smiled broadly at one another.

"We did it!" Lucy and Elana both shouted happily. They had just accomplished an amazing feat. Together, they looked out from the center of the bridge, taking in the landscape of the incredible mountains and the valley between them. After several minutes, Lucy and Elana headed across the gold side of the bridge, back toward the fuchsia castle.

Chapter Eleven

"I'm so glad you came!" Elana said to Lucy. "I was really scared. I thought I would never get back."

"Why did you leave in the first place?"

"Oh. I feel awful. I was mad at my dad because he never let me go anywhere. I don't have any sisters or brothers, so wandering around the castle gets really boring with no one to play with. I decided I needed an adventure."

"Your dad thinks you abandoned him and that you hate him," Lucy said.

Elana's eyes watered up. "That's not it at all! I love him very much, but he never let me go anywhere because he thought it was unsafe. I just felt so trapped and bored in our castle. I never meant to be gone for so long. I thought if I just slipped out one night and came back a few days later, he would never notice. He's always so busy."

"I know how that is," Lucy nodded knowingly. "My parents are doctors."

Elana looked at her with curiosity. "Is that like a warlock?"

"Er, kind of. They help people and they are gone a lot. So I just mean that I understand. That's how I ended up here too."

"Where are you from?" Elana asked.

"A different realm," Lucy replied.

"You mean the Land of the Forest?"

"No, like a totally different realm. It's a long story. I live in a place called London."

"That sounds pretty. Maybe I can visit you someday."

Lucy smiled. The two girls reached the peak overlooking Elana's kingdom. Right where the path down began, there was a fork. They could go down the one Lucy came up, or try and hike down the extra steep one. Elana looked at Lucy nervously, "Shall we go the long route?"

"I don't think so. We might run into these things that tried to eat me."

"I think you mean mastilors. Yes, they are vicious. I'm impressed you escaped them!"

"Hmm. I have an idea," said Lucy. She took out her golden loom, sparkling hook, and a bag of magic bands.

Elana looked on curiously, watching Lucy build four long figures. "What are those?"

"Skis!" Lucy beamed. She helped Elana into the skis, and they each grabbed branches from the kaleidoscopic trees to use as poles. "This is going to be *really* steep. The skis will take us down the mountain a million times faster than if we hiked down, and it will be so much fun!"

Elana looked at Lucy as if she had gone completely mad. "I—I don't think I can do that."

"Did you or did you not just build a giant bridge across a set of mountains that could have sent you plummeting to your death in a deep valley below?" Lucy prompted her.

"Well, yes. But what if we hit a tree?"

"I checked it out already—these trees have healing powers!" Lucy assured her.

Elana wasn't convinced that driving straight into a tree was something that could be healed like a scratch, but she nodded anyway.

"Elana, you go first and wrap this cord around your waist. If anything happens, I can help you." Elana nodded again, winced, and began to slide down the mountain.

"Hey, this isn't so bad." She smiled at Lucy as she began to pick up speed. "Wait! Aren't you coming? Lucy!"

Lucy laughed and hopped on her skis, following Elana down the mountain. The two girls weaved back and forth along the steep trail. Lucy could see Elana speeding uncontrollably, looking like she was going to fall. She tugged gently on the cord, righting Elana in the process.

As they headed down the mountain, the trail took an unexpected turn. Lucy remembered the trail appearing straight down the mountain when she had seen it earlier, but this was heading in an entirely different direction. Off in the distance, Lucy saw something she did not expect: the cliff face. They were headed straight for it! She tried to slow down, but the mountain was so steep that there was no stopping them from careening off the cliff. Unless she wanted to get up close and personal with one of the trees, and that was not an option.

Very quickly, Elana came to the same realization. She started to shout, waving her arms back at Lucy to signal her. But Lucy was already on it. She grabbed her loom from her bag as she let the skis do the work. She wrapped the bands tightly around the magic loom with supernatural quickness, and slid the finished product down to Elana along the cord that connected them. She repeated the process for herself, and strapped it to her back.

"When you head over the cliff, pull the cord!" Lucy yelled to Elana. Lucy sped up, reaching the same area as Elana just as the cliff was approaching. The two girls nodded at one another, and with confidence, they soared off the cliff. Each girl pulled her cord, and the magic loom parachutes that Lucy had woven came popping out. The parachutes opened, and the girls felt a big tug as they caught the air, slowing them from their plunge.

"This is amazing!" Elana shouted to Lucy, with her bright green parachute over her head. Lucy smiled back from beneath her own blue canopy, and the two girls floated down from the cliff face by the gates to the kingdom.

Chapter Twelve

Elana and Lucy landed with a thump at the edge of the kingdom gates. They stood up and dusted themselves off, smiling from ear to ear at the excitement they had just had.

"That was so much fun!" Elana said, bursting with happiness. Lucy didn't answer. "Lucy, didn't you have fun? What's wrong?"

Lucy was staring through the gates, a look of horror on her face. "Elana . . . the fields."

Elana looked at her once beautiful fields, but they were scorched. Green goo sopped from the trees, and there was charred fruit scattered about. "What happened?" she cried, running into a row of an orchard.

"Elana, wait! Be careful!" Lucy yelled to her as she ran to catch up.

"But, but my kingdom! What happened? Why is everything destroyed?"

"It looks like the Horned Orogawg was here. That's its green goo," Lucy pointed out. She felt terrible. They hadn't even arrived back at the castle yet. This was supposed to be an incredible day. Lucy had fulfilled her promise and found Elana. They had accomplished so much, and now everything looked bleak and terrible.

Elana wiped away tears as she knelt down and looked at the broken earth. "We have to go back to the castle right now; I need to make sure my father is okay!" Lucy nodded and took Elana's hand as they began to carefully walk through the devastated fields. She was worried about Alyssa now, too. They passed through the damaged fruit trees and came upon the field of pinwheel flowers. Lucy winced as she started to enter, fearing another storm of violet tornadoes and whizzing razor-sharp flowers. "What are you doing? Do you have a death wish?" Elana pulled Lucy back from the field.

"I—I thought this was the way back to the castle. Is there another way?" Lucy asked.

"Of course there is. You can't go *through* the meadow. It's meant to protect the castle,"

Elana explained. "Come this way." They walked around the perimeter of the pinwheel meadow to another just beside it. "Fire blossoms— they're my favorite. We have some in our garden, too!" Ahead of them was a meadow of flowers of every color that let off flickering lights like a whole field of sparklers. Elana gestured for Lucy to stand in front of one particularly large fire blossom, and she stood at the one next to her.

"On three, we both pick up our flowers. Got it?" Elana said seriously to Lucy.

"Got it." Lucy lowered her hand around the stem of the flower, waiting for Elana's count.

"One, two, *three.*" They both picked their fire blossoms at the same time, and the sparkling lights glowed, becoming double their original size. Slowly, the flowers rose from the ground, lifting Lucy and Elana high into the air. The spraying sparks glittered all around them, and the girls were carried over the dangerous pinwheel meadow by the stems of the fire blossoms. Lucy looked in awe as they went over the vast field, smiling at Elana as they went. She realized this was what the king must have meant for her to do when he told her about Elana's favorite flowers. Why hadn't he just said so it in the first place?

They came to the edge of the pinwheel meadow and their floating fire blossoms lowered them gently onto the ground. They landed, and began walking toward the fuchsia castle. Elana and Lucy looked around for any sign of the king or Alyssa, but everything was eerily quiet.

They walked up the steps of the crystal castle and went inside. Elana and Lucy went through all of the main rooms, and up the stairs. They called out for the king and Alyssa, but they were nowhere to be found. Elana beckoned Lucy to a small doorway by the staircase. "We'll go up to one of the towers. Maybe we can see something from up high," she said. They climbed the winding stairs to the central tower of the castle. Just as Lucy thought she wouldn't be able to climb another step, they arrived at a doorway. Elana turned the handle, and the door clicked open.

Peering out off the balcony, Elana and Lucy squinted across the landscape. There was no sign of the others! Frustrated and hopeless, Lucy looked down at one of the rooftops below. It was the roof where the king had landed his chariot. "Look!" shrieked Lucy. "They're inside the chariot!" Just below, the king and Alyssa were cowered in the winged chariot, looking like they were hiding. Elana and Lucy rushed down the tower staircase and to the entrance of the rooftop. They bolted out of the doorway and reached the chariot. The king jumped out, scooped up Elana, and twirled her around.

"My precious daughter! You've come home!" The bearded king had tears in his eyes.

"Daddy, I missed you!" Elana hugged her father tightly and didn't let go for a long time.

"Sweetheart, come into the chariot. You're just in time. We were hoping you would be back, but we were afraid we would have to leave without you," the king said earnestly.

"Where are we going? What happened to the fruit fields?" Elana urged.

"The Horned Orogawg came into our land just after Lucy left to find you. It normally stays within the confines of the Volcan Trail and protects us, but something went wrong. It entered our kingdom, and in the process destroyed much of our land. We must leave before it attacks everything in sight."

"But where will we go? This is our home!" Elana began to get upset.

"I don't know, maybe the mountains. We just can't stay here," the king said, worriedly. "What do you think, Lucy?" No one answered. The king turned and Lucy and Alyssa were hugging tightly, smiling with tears running down their cheeks. "Oh, right. Lucy, I cannot express the gratitude I have for your bringing my daughter home." Lucy turned to him, listening. "I understand if you need to leave now, since you have fulfilled your promise. Elana and I will find a way out of this on our own. I can show you back through the volcano entrance so you can return to where you came from."

"Don't be ridiculous," Alyssa and Lucy chimed in unison. "We'll figure it out together!" Just as Lucy was starting to feel confident, something dripped on her shoulder.

"Lucy!" Alyssa smacked her shoulder with great speed, flicking something off. "Ouch!" Alyssa's hand was burned, and the spot on Lucy's shoulder smoldered. It was the green goo! They looked up, and atop the high tower was the Horned Orogawg, glaring down at them.

"Quick! Get in the chariot!" The king yelled, helping all three of the girls into the winged chariot. He jumped in and the chariot lifted from the ground. They flew up and around the castle, as the Horned Orogawg jumped from tower to tower, shattering whole sections of the castle's beautiful pink crystals as it went. "We should be okay, because the monster cannot fly," the king said, confidently.

The next instant, the Horned Orogawg shot a stream of green goo at the chariot, missing it by inches. Lucy, Alyssa, and Elana all shot looks at the king—the monster might not be able to fly, but he could still shoot them out of the sky. The king veered the chariot over the pinwheel field and above the scorched fruit orchards. On the earth below, Lucy could see a glowing orb close to the ground.

"Quick! Get to the light!"

"Lucy, now is not the time to land on the ground. The Horned Orogawg could get to us!" the king proclaimed.

"Please, I think I know what's wrong. Just bring us over there." Reluctantly, the king followed Lucy's instructions and headed toward the glowing orb. He landed the chariot in the field, and each of the girls slowly climbed out.

Alyssa and Elana followed closely behind Lucy, their gold hair blowing in the wind. Lucy crouched down next to the glowing orb. It was the butterfly she had created to distract the monster! But it looked like it was dying. There was ash covering much of the orb. "The butterfly was the only thing that kept the Horned Orogawg calm! Maybe the volcano was a bad place for it to live." They all watched in worry as the butterfly in the orb stopped glowing.

Just then, the ground began to quake. "Oh no!" shouted Alyssa. "The Horned Orogawg is coming! Lucy, get your loom! Do something!"

"I—I can't! I've run out of magic bands!" Lucy looked to Elana in terror. Neither of them had any more bands to help save themselves. The monster was coming closer, spraying the deadly green goo in its path. Any remaining trees in the field made a loud popping noise and quickly exploded, sending charred and demolished fruit flying. The monster came directly in front of them, and kneeled down in front of the dark orb.

Then, the Horned Orogawg began to cry.

"I think he's sad," Elana said.

"Elana, stay back. He might be still now, but he could spray you at any moment," her father said. Just as the king finished his sentence, the Horned Orogawg looked up. Its dark eyes squinted in despair and anger, and he bared his teeth. He began to growl and wail, and looked like he was preparing to shoot his fiery goo at them. The king turned his back to the monster, covering the three girls with his cloak to shield them.

Lucy, Alyssa, and Elana all hugged each other under the king's cloak. "It's been nice knowing you!" cried Elana.

"Lucy, you were the best friend I ever had!" whimpered Alyssa.

"I love you both!" added Lucy, as they hugged each other tighter.

A few moments passed. And another few moments. And another few moments. The girls all looked at each other, wondering why nothing was happening. Lucy peeked under the king's cloak in the direction of the monster. The Horned Orogawg was turned away from them, staring up at the sky. Lucy, Alyssa, Elana, and the king all stood up, cautiously looking for what it was the monster was seeing.

Off in the distance, a glowing cloud approached. As it came closer, Lucy could see that it was not a cloud at all, but hundreds of small glowing orbs. The closer they came, the more color Lucy could see. "Butterflies!" she shouted. They looked at each other in wonder.

"It's true!" Alyssa said. "But where did they come from? I thought you ran out of magic bands."

"We did!" said Lucy and Elana. They all watched as the beautiful magic butterflies came bobbing into the field. They settled all around the monster, who sat down in the dirt. He rested his head on the ground, letting one of the orbs rest on his nose.

"I think he's happy!" said the king.

"I still don't understand where they came from. This isn't possible. Don't you have to have a magic loom to make the butterflies? They aren't natural here," Alyssa pointed out.

"Look!" Elana pointed to the gates of the kingdom. There was a crowd entering. "Who could it be? No one ever comes here from the outside!"

Lucy jumped for joy, "It's my friends from the Land of the Forest!" And so it was! At the front, she saw the colorful zebras leading a herd of animals from the other side of the realm.

When they arrived at the fruit field to meet Lucy and the others, the first zebra gave Lucy a big smile. "Hello, friend. I never thought I would see you again."

"I know! I thought you said you would never come here!" Lucy chimed.

"It's true, we of the Land of the Forest never planned on such a journey. But our messenger—the bird who gave you the silver loom for the princess—reported back to us that this kingdom was not solely a place of danger and volcanic activity. It seems we were mistaken, and this kingdom is a beautiful land like our own."

Lucy and Elana looked at one another with wide eyes. "So how did you get here if you didn't come from the Volcan Trail?" Lucy asked.

The zebra smiled. "Lucy, your effort to save the princess served more than just one purpose. In building the bridge together, you have connected our worlds. You have done us a great service, so now we in the Land of the Forest and those in the Kingdom of the Fuchsia Castle can be in harmony. We can travel between the two kingdoms and work with one another for a more peaceful realm."

Lucy and Elana were dumbfounded. From behind the group, the king came forward and greeted the zebras. With tears in his eyes, he bowed to the animals. "I am so happy to know that our kingdoms can finally be united in friendship." The zebras kneeled, bowing in agreement.

The king turned to the three girls and hugged them. "I'm so happy that everyone is safe!" Just then, they heard a growl. They all turned in panic, looking at the Horned Orogawg. To their relief, he was just playing with one of the butterfly orbs.

"How did you know to send the butterflies?" Lucy asked the animals.

"Lucy, butterflies are often used in our world to express beauty and bring calm to those who are restless," explained a zebra. The magical animals behind her all nodded knowingly.

"Oh . . . I didn't know that," Lucy grumbled, realizing her magic had not been unique.

Alyssa grinned. "It's okay. We still think you're special!" And all three friends laughed.

"We will just have to make sure the Horned Orogawg always has his friends nearby so that this kind of destruction never happens again," said the king. "It will take some time, but we will regrow our fields and repair the castle."

The zebras looked at one another, communicating with just their eyes. "You will not be alone in this. The animals of the Land of the Forest will help you rebuild." Looking humbled and grateful, the king thanked them.

Alyssa and Lucy looked at one another in sadness. With tears in her eyes, Alyssa said, "We won't be able to help. I have to go home to America."

Lucy looked at her feet, "And I have to go home to London."

"I knew you would say that," Elana groaned. "I don't want you to leave."

The king came over and knelt down, meeting their eyes. "You will always have a place here. You saved my daughter and reminded us that the strangers beyond our borders can be our friends. I will be forever grateful to you both." The king hugged both Lucy and Alyssa. The girls nodded, and readied themselves to leave.

Lucy and Alyssa said their farewells to the animals from the Land of the Forest. The king gestured to his chariot. "You mean we don't have to walk back through the mountains or the Volcan Trail?" asked Lucy.

"Of course not. We will take you." The king smiled.

They all hopped into the chariot and waved to the animals in the field, even the Horned Orogawg. The chariot raised into the air, and the girls all held hands as they soared over the kingdom, over the mountains, past the bridge, and into the Land of the Forest.

The chariot landed softly by the old fir tree with the green door. They all jumped out, and Lucy, Alyssa, and Elana stood in a triangle, staring at one another. Lucy sighed and said, "Well, I guess we better get going."

"Wait!" Alyssa chimed. "Look what I found!" She pulled out a bag of ordinary purple rubber bands from her pocket.

Lucy smiled and took the bands. She pulled out her loom from her bag, and with the regular bands she wove three bracelets. She put one on her own wrist, one on Alyssa's, and another on Elana's.

"What kind of magic do these bands do?" asked Elana.

"Friendship," said Alyssa.

"Where does it say that?"

"It doesn't, but we know it's there," said Lucy. They smiled and gave each other one last big hug. The king opened the door of the fir tree and waved goodbye as Alyssa and Lucy passed through.

Chapter Thirteen

Everything was dark—Lucy's eyes were tightly shut, and something was poking into her side. She opened her eyes, and saw the room full of books strewn about and the fallen bookcase. She pulled a heavy medical text out from underneath her. "Ow," she groaned, as she cast the book aside. Lucy turned and saw Alyssa wide-eyed and beaming.

"I cannot believe that was real!" Alyssa squealed.

"What was real? Alyssa, the bookcase fell on you and you have been knocked out for hours. What are you talking about?" Lucy said seriously.

Alyssa's face fell. "Oh. I—I thought we were . . . that we went . . ."

Lucy held up her wrist showing Alyssa her matching purple friendship bracelet and burst out laughing. "Just kidding!"

"Lucy! You terrified me! I thought I had gone mad!" Lucy giggled and they both sat up from the floor.

"Well, on a serious note, I am so sorry you got kidnapped," said Lucy.

"And I'm so sorry that I started this whole mess in the first place," Alyssa added.

"No, I think it was all worth it. We had an adventure we will never forget!" The friends beamed at each other. "Oh no! Alyssa! What time is it?"

Alyssa blanched. "My flight!" They both jumped up and looked around the disastrous room.

"We need to clean this up, and quick!" Lucy looked out the window and saw her mum and dad getting out of their car in the driveway. "Help! Go to the other side of the bookshelf." Alyssa went to one side and knelt down. "Ready? One, two, three!" Alyssa and Lucy heaved the bookshelf up and slammed it back against the wall.

"Lucy! We're home!" Lucy heard her mother call from the first floor.

"The books!" The girls shoved the books back onto the shelves as rapidly as they could and then bolted down the two flights of stairs. They skidded into the kitchen and Lucy shoved a chocolate biscuit into her mouth as her mother walked in, shuffling through the post.

"Hi, Mum!" Lucy choked.

"Lucy, good heavens where are you manners? Are you okay? You look dreadful." Her mum put her arms around Lucy and gave her a kiss on the forehead.

"I'm fine!" Lucy blurted.

"Hello, girls!" Dr. Stillwater came bounding into the kitchen. "Looks like it's time to send Alyssa off to the airport. Where's Abigail?"

"I'm right here," Abigail smiled her twinkly smile as she came in from the living room. "I'm sorry, girls. I must have fallen asleep. Did your tea get cold?"

"It's great!" Alyssa and Lucy chimed in unison. Abigail, Dr. Smith, and Dr. Stillwater all looked at the girls in amusement.

"Do you have your things all packed and ready, Alyssa?" asked Lucy's mum.

"Yes ma'am," Alyssa gestured to Lucy to help her with her bag.

The girls darted out of the room guiltily and grabbed Alyssa's things. They headed out to the car, with Dr. Stillwater and Dr. Smith closely behind. As Dr. Stillwater lifted Alyssa's suitcase into the trunk of the car, Lucy and Abigail looked across the street. Mrs. Gloucester was standing in the window, grinning knowingly and waving. Lucy and Alyssa giggled and waved back before they jumped into the car and headed to the airport.

As they arrived at security, Lucy and Alyssa gave each other extra long hugs. Alyssa started to turn away to get into line, but Lucy ran after her. She grabbed Alyssa's wrist, and this time, she tied her bracelet extra tight.